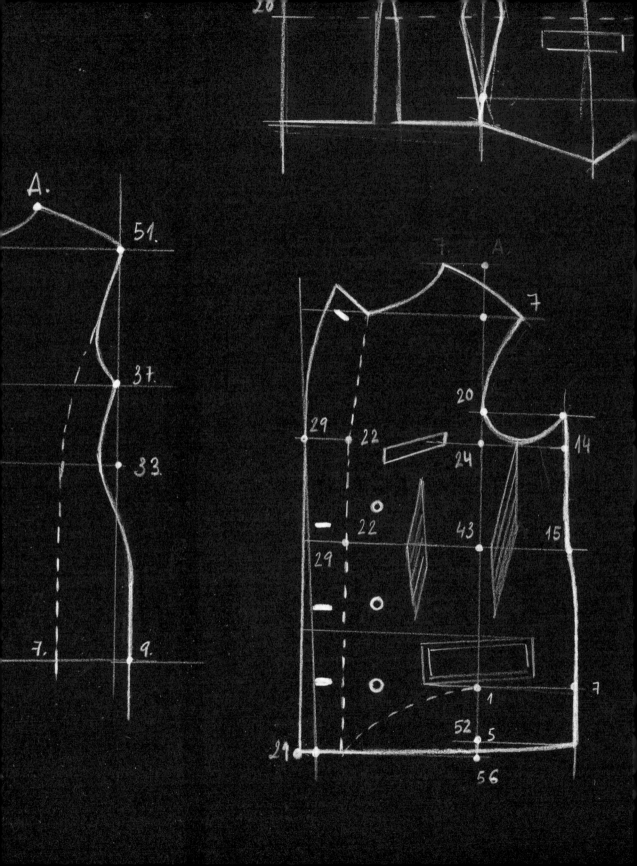

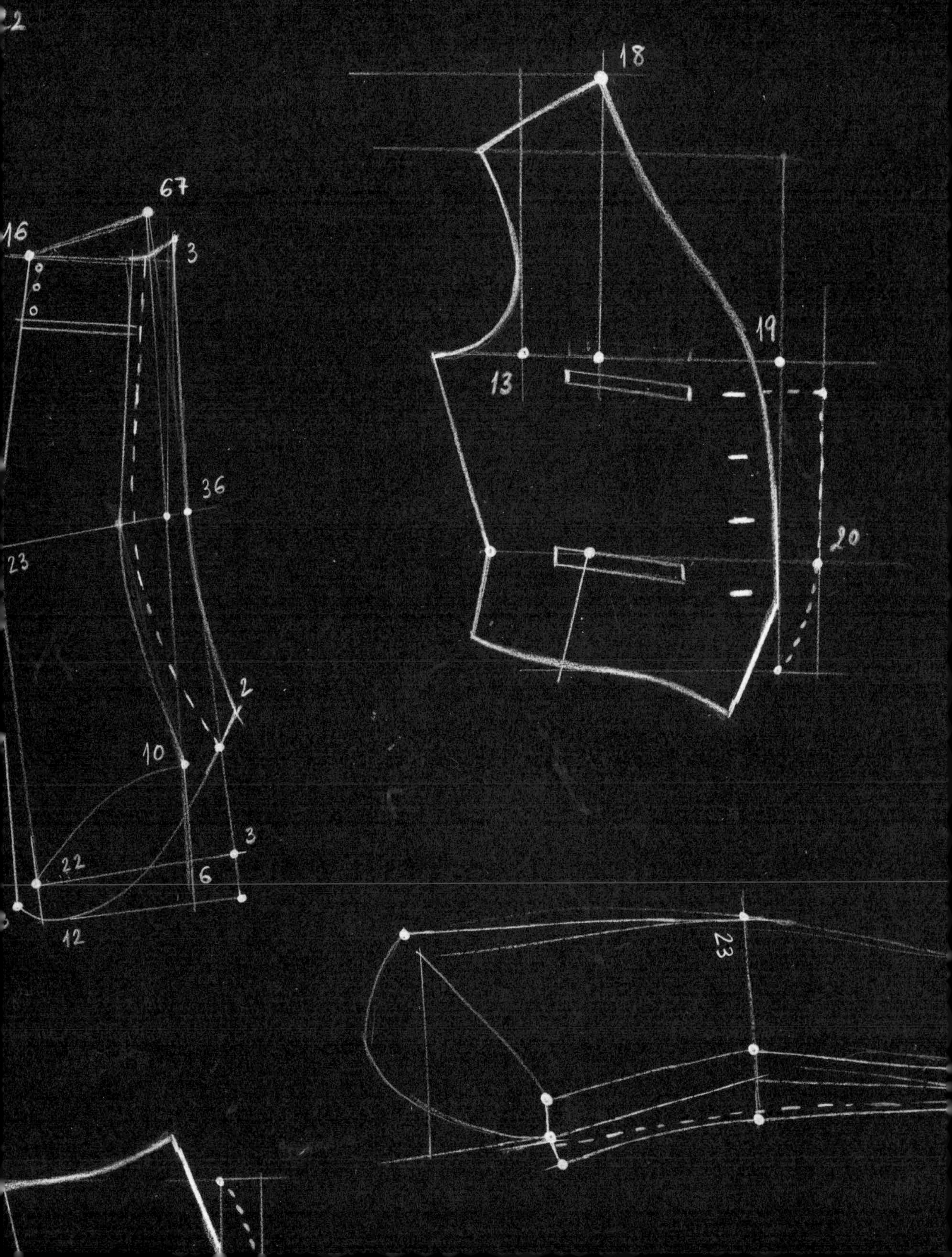
18
67
16
3
19
13
36
20
23
2
10
3
22
6
12
23

Originally published in 2019
by Bruaá Editora, Portugal,
as *A Manta do José*

First published in the UK in 2021
by Green Bean Books
c/o Pen & Sword Books Ltd
47 Church Street, Barnsley,
South Yorkshire, S70 2AS
www.greenbeanbooks.com

Designed by Ian Hughes, www.mousematdesign.com
Edited by Kate Baker and Phoebe Jascourt
Production by Hugh Allan

Printed in China by Imago
012132.9K1/B1613/A6

FSC
MIX
Paper from
responsible sources
www.fsc.org   FSC® C005748

Green
Bean
Books

BENJY'S BLANKET

ADAPTED BY MIGUEL GOUVEIA AND ILLUSTRATED BY RAQUEL CATALINA

When Benjy was born, his grandad, who was a tailor,
made a beautiful blanket for his cradle.

Benjy loved the blanket more than his grandad could have ever imagined. Long after he had learned to walk and talk, Benjy still refused to part with it. He was never seen without his grandad's gift.

One day, when his mother saw the wrinkled, dirty blanket, she said, "Benjy, it's time to throw this old thing away!"

"I'll never throw it away!" Benjy replied. "Grandad gave me this blanket. Now it's my cape, and I need it to fly. Here I go!" he cried, as he zoomed through the house.

Later that day, Benjy flew into Grandad's shop and asked him if there was anything he could do to fix the blanket.

Grandad picked it up, looked at it again and again, turned it around and around, and said, "You know, Benjy, I think we still have enough good material to make you a jacket."

Grandad started to measure, cut, and sew, measure, cut, and sew, measure, cut, and sew. When he had finished, Benjy had a new jacket that fit him like a glove.

How Benjy loved that jacket! He wore it every day. But, like every child, Benjy grew bigger, while his jacket, like any jacket, stayed the same size. It became much too small for him, and the more Benjy wore it, the shabbier it got.

One day, his mother looked at him and said, "Benjy! That jacket! It's going in the rag bag right now!"

"No, it's not!" Benjy cried. "This jacket was made for me by Grandad. I'll talk to him, and he'll know what to do."

Benjy took the jacket to his grandad and asked him to save it from disappearing into his mother's big sack of old clothes.

Grandad picked it up, looked at it again and again, turned it around and around, and said, "You know, Benjy, I think we still have enough good material here to make you a vest."

Grandad started to measure, cut, and sew, measure, cut, and sew. When he had finished, Benjy put on his small vest and a big smile.

But as time went on, Benjy's vest – besides having acquired a big collection of stains – seemed to have more holes than fabric.

When his mother saw the crumpled, moth-eaten garment, she said, "Benjy, that vest has done its job. We have to get rid of it."

"That's not true!" Benjy replied. "Grandad can still turn it into something new. You'll see. He's the best tailor in the world."

When Grandad opened the door, Benjy gave him the vest without saying a word. Grandad smiled, picked it up, looked at it again and again, turned it around and around, and said, "You know, Benjy, I think we still have enough good material here to make you a scarf."

So Grandad started to measure, cut, and sew. When he had finished, he put the scarf around Benjy's neck.

Time passed, and the scarf became so worn out that it barely resembled a scarf at all.

One day, when Benjy's mother saw the scarf, all torn and tattered, she said, "Benjy, I'm sorry, but this really needs to be thrown away now."

"Don't even think about it!" Benjy protested. "I know it doesn't look like it, but that's the scarf that Grandad made me. I'll talk to him, and he'll know what to do."

Benjy went to Grandad's shop and took what was left of the scarf out of his pocket. Carefully, Grandad picked it up, looked at it again and again, turned it around and around, and said, "You know, I think we still have enough good material here to make you a button." And that is what he did.

Benjy pulled the button off his trousers and asked Grandad to sew the new one there so that everyone could see it.

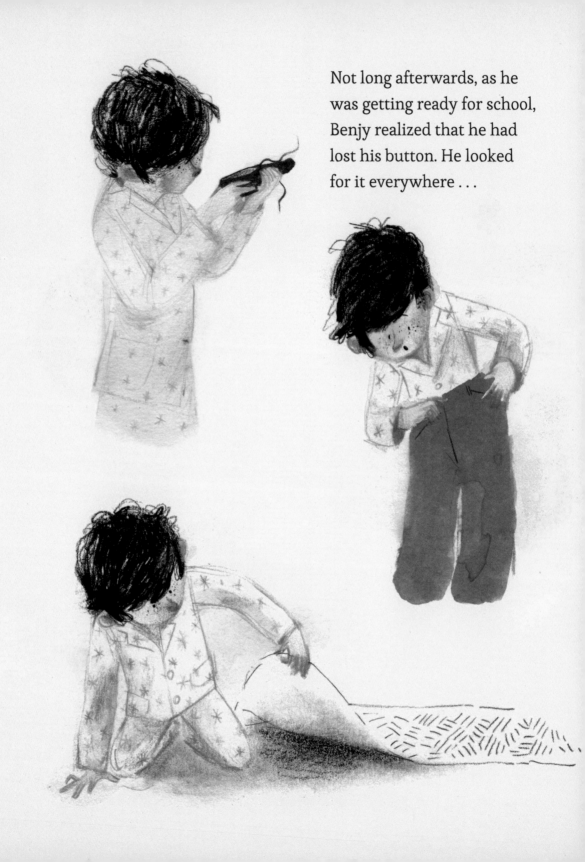

Not long afterwards, as he was getting ready for school, Benjy realized that he had lost his button. He looked for it everywhere . . .

but there was no sign of it.

"Benjy," said his mother. "What can Grandad do with nothing?"

"I'm not sure," Benjy replied sadly, "but Grandad always knows what to do."

This time, Grandad said nothing when Benjy told him what had happened.

Benjy was puzzled, but he waited patiently. He recognized the look on Grandad's face. He could see that Grandad was once again measuring, cutting, and sewing in his mind, thinking about what to do.

Soon Grandad broke the silence and said, "You know, Benjy, maybe that button was not the end after all. I think we still have enough good material here to make . . .

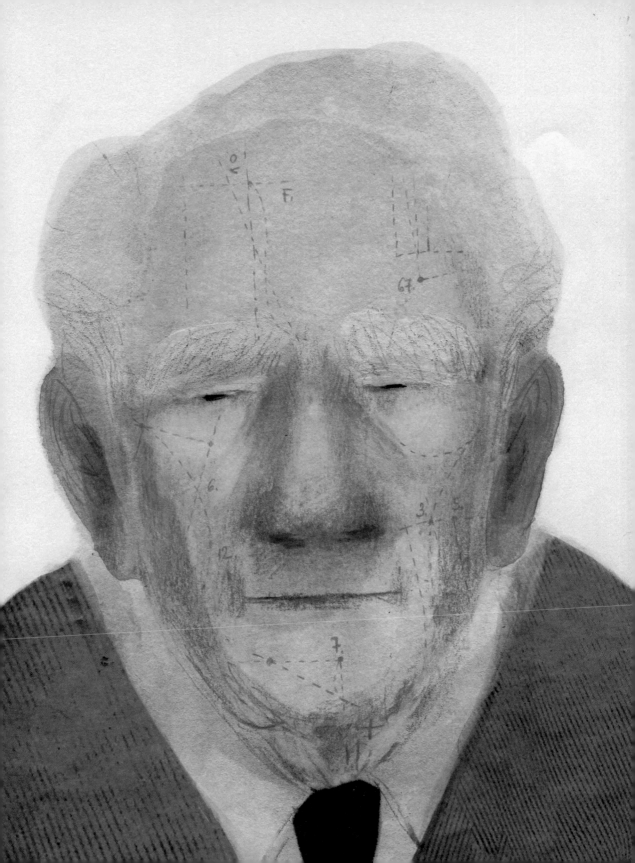

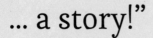

... a story!"

Grandad gave Benjy a pencil and a notepad. Together they sat down to write. Their story started like this:

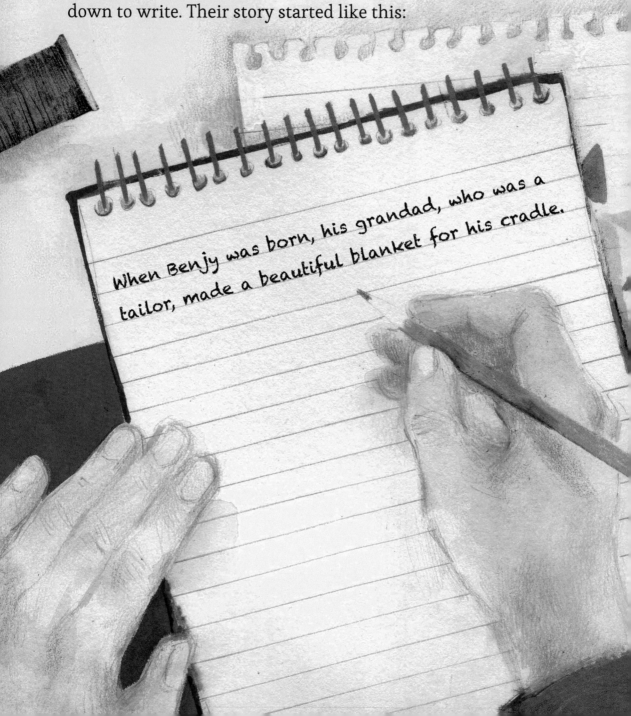

When Benjy was born, his grandad, who was a tailor, made a beautiful blanket for his cradle.

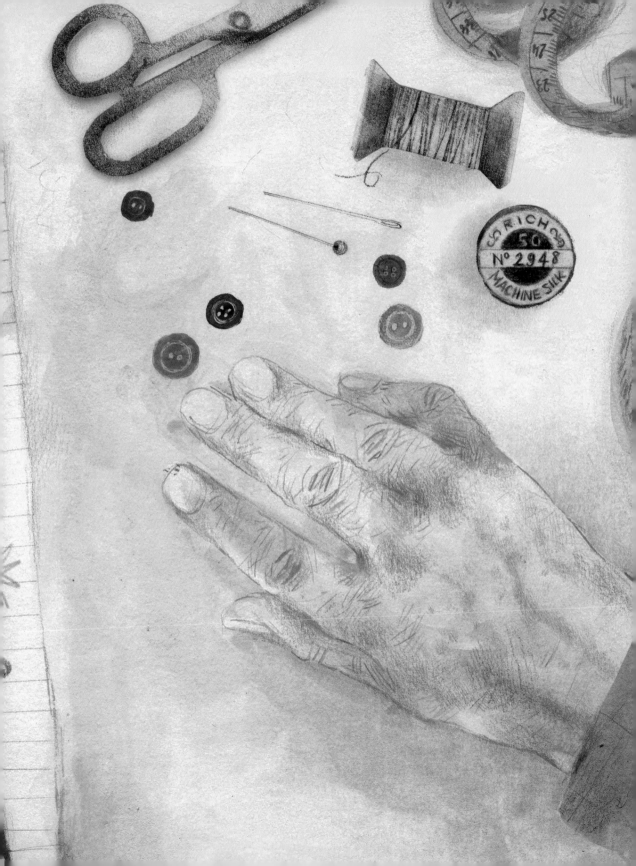

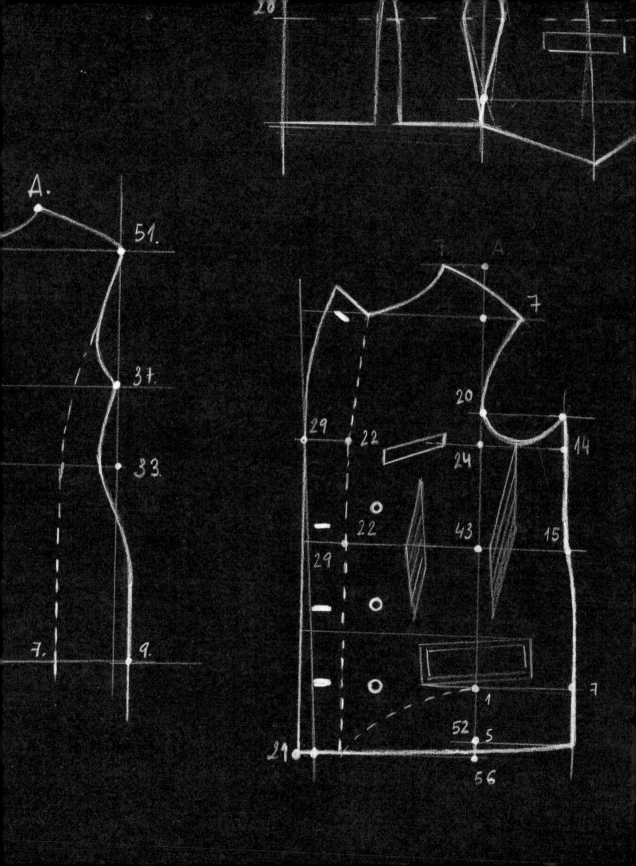

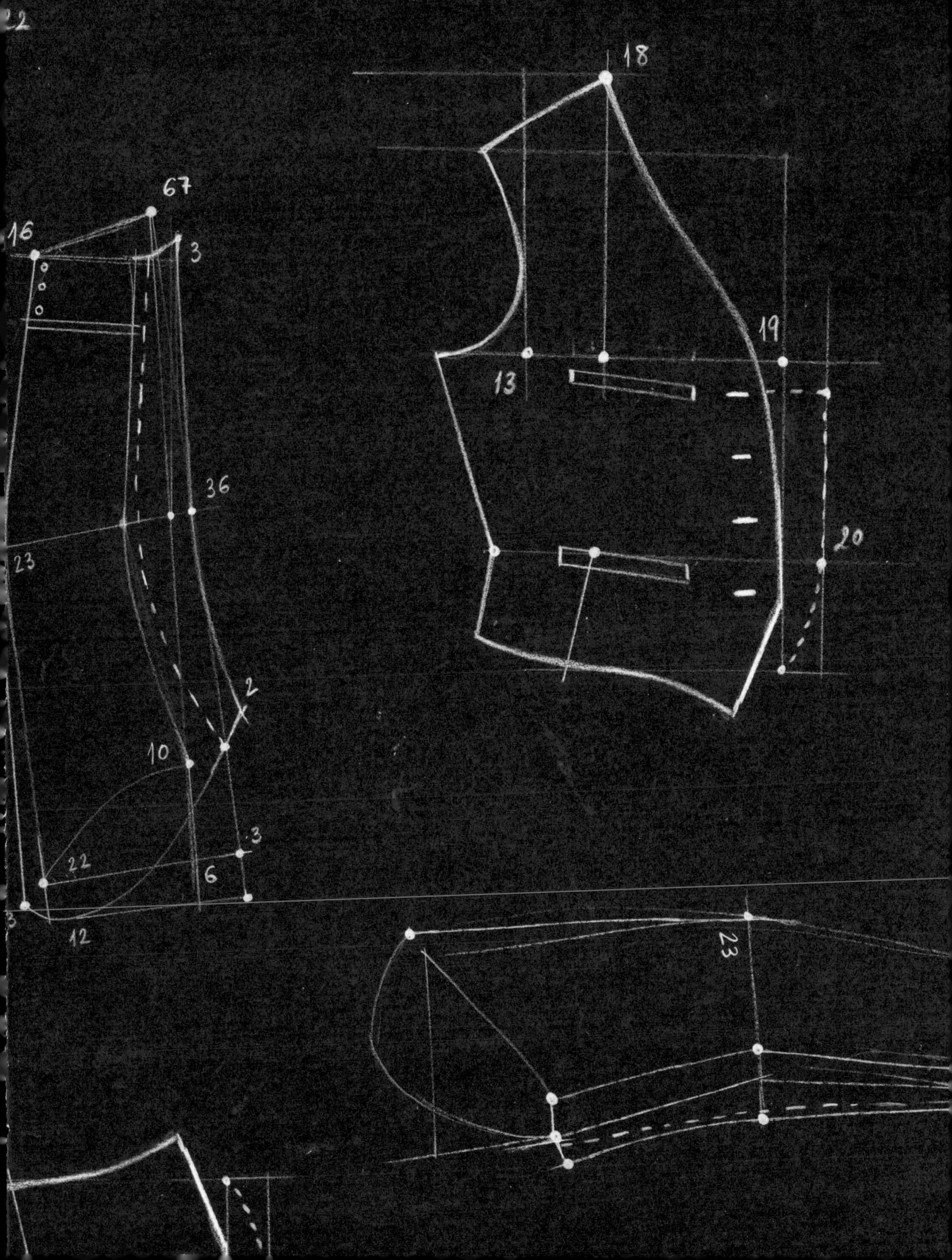
22
18
67
16
3
13
19
36
20
23
2
10
3
22
6
12
23